Spells

Emily Gribbitt

Macmillan Children's Books

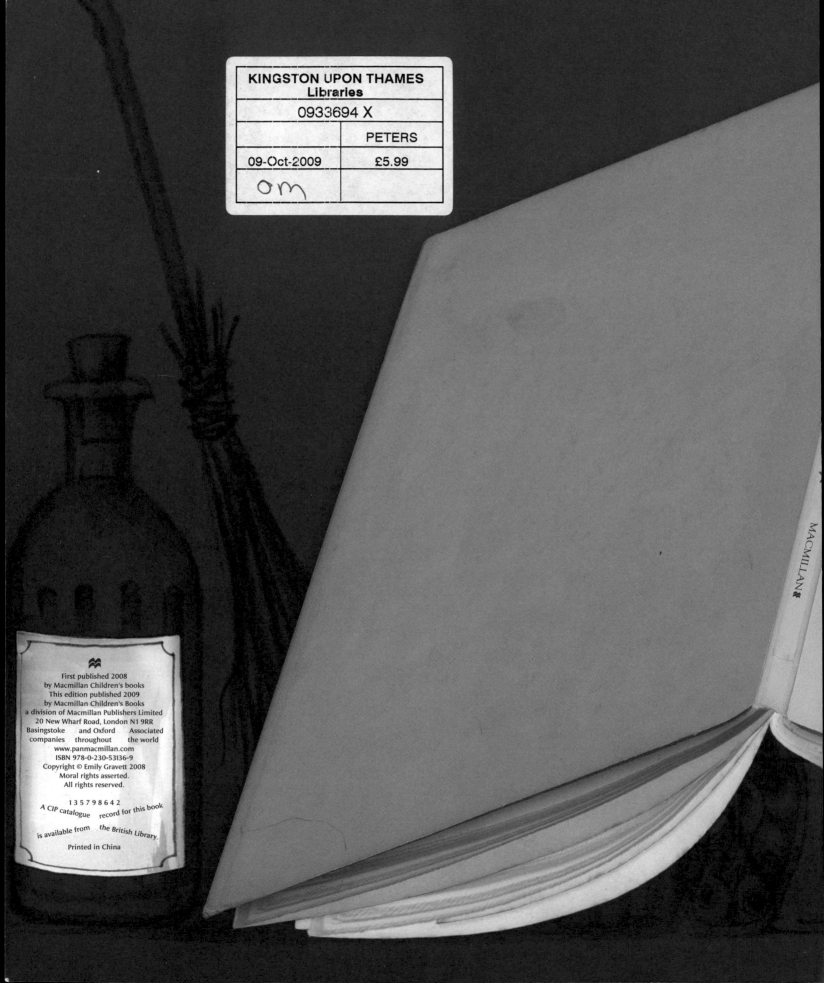

MACMILLAN

First published 2008
by Macmillan Children's books
This edition published 2009
by Macmillan Children's Books
a division of Macmillan Publishers Limited
20 New Wharf Road, London N1 9RR
Basingstoke   and Oxford   Associated
companies   throughout   the world
www.panmacmillan.com
ISBN 978-0-230-53136-9
Copyright © Emily Gravett 2008
Moral rights asserted.
All rights reserved.

1 3 5 7 9 8 6 4 2
A CIP catalogue   record for this book

is available from   the British Library.

Printed in China

SPELLS

Emily Gribbitt

MACMILLAN CHILDREN'S BOOKS

There was once a frog who found a book.
He wished it was a book about boats
and that he was a pirate sailing the seven seas.

But it was just an old book of spells, and he was just a small green frog.

He wished it was a book about castles
and that he was a handsome prince kissing a beautiful princess.

But it was just an old book of spells, and he was still just a small green frog.

Then Frog had an idea . . .

Spell
to become a
Handsome Prince

Into
the cauldron
these words cast

Hocus

Croakus

Carrotozabbit

Stir three times and out spells . . .

At last!
Frog was tall.
He was handsome.
He was a prince!

And he was going to kiss
a beautiful princess.

It was magic.
And he was . . .

. . . just a small green frog (again).

SMALL PRINT
Please read carefully

Handsome Prince Spell® will be reversed
upon the kiss of a genuine princess

There was once a frog who wished he could read another book by Emily Gravett. Then he discovered that he could!

LITTLE MOUSE'S
~~Emily Gravett's~~
Big Book
of Fears

ISBN: 978-0-230-01619-4

The
Rabbit Problem
by
Emily Gravett
(and a lot of rabbits)

🥕 + 🥕 = 2

34
55 +
89

ISBN: 978-0-230-70423-7